HELLO! WELCOME TO THE FABUMOUSE WORLD OF THE THEA SISTERS!

Thea Sisters

Hi, I'm Thea Stilton, Geronimo Stilton's sister! I am a special reporter for <u>The Rodent's Gazette</u>, the most famouse newspaper on Mouse Island. I love traveling and meeting new mice all over the world, like the Thea Sisters. These five friends have helped me out with my adventures. Let me introduce you to these fabumouse young mice!

Colette has a real passion for fashion. She loves to design her own clothes in her favorite color, pink.

Violet loves studying and learning new things. She is a fan of classical music and dreams of becoming a famous violinist someday.

Pamela loves pizza so much she eats it for breakfast. She is a skilled mechanic who can fix just about any motor she gets her paws on.

PAULINA is shy and loves to read about faraway places. But she loves traveling to those places even more.

Nicky is from the Australian Outback, where she developed a love of nature and the environment. This outdoors-loving mouse is always on the move.

Thea Sisters

Thea Stilton

MOUSEFORD ACADEMY

THE MYSTERIOUS LOVE LETTER

Scholastic Inc.

Copyright © 2010 by Edizioni Piemme S.p.A., Palazzo Mondadori, Via Mondadori 1, 20090 Segrate, Italy. International Rights © Atlantyca S.p.A. English translation © 2016 by Atlantyca S.p.A.

The publisher does not have any control over and does not assume any responsibility for author or third-party websites or their content.

GERONIMO STILTON and THEA STILTON names, characters, and related indicia are copyright, trademark, and exclusive license of Atlantyca S.p.A. All rights reserved. The moral right of the author has been asserted. Based on an original idea by Elisabetta Dami.

www.geronimostilton.com

Published by Scholastic Inc., 557 Broadway, New York, NY 10012. SCHOLASTIC and associated logos are trademarks and/or registered trademarks of Scholastic Inc.

Stilton is the name of a famous English cheese. It is a registered trademark of the Stilton Cheese Makers' Association. For more information, go to www.stiltoncheese.com.

No part of this publication may be reproduced, stored in a retrieval system, or transmitted in any form or by any means, electronic, mechanical, photocopying, recording, or otherwise, without written permission of the copyright holder. For information regarding permission, please contact: Atlantyca S.p.A., Via Leopardi 8, 20123 Milan, Italy; e-mail foreignrights@atlantyca.it, www.atlantyca.com.

This book is a work of fiction. Names, characters, places, and incidents are either the product of the author's imagination or are used fictitiously, and any resemblance to actual persons, living or dead, business establishments, events, or locales is entirely coincidental.

ISBN 978-9-386-04107-4

Text by Thea Stilton
Original title *Una misteriosa lettera d'amore*
Cover by Giuseppe Facciotto
Illustrations by Chiara Balleello (pencils) and Francesco Castelli (color)
Graphics by Yuko Egusa

Special thanks to Beth Dunfey
Translated by Anna Pizzelli
Interior design by Kevin Callahan / BNGO Books
First printing, 2016
Reprinted by Scholastic India Pvt. Ltd., 2016, 2017(Twice), 2018
Printed at MicroPrints (India), New Delhi

A SECRET ADMIRER

The air in Mouseford Academy's newsroom was filled with *TENSION*. The latest issue of the school's weekly paper was about to go to *press*, but the front-page articles were not ready!

That morning, a few mouselets and ratlets had met to edit the sports *section*. Now it was late afternoon, and they were finishing up.

It was time for Tanja, the paper's editor in chief, to take over. "*Good luck, team*," called Ryder Flashyfur, the paper's sports editor, on his way out.

Tanja and the rest of her

Good luck!

editorial team—Colette, Nicky, Pamela, Paulina, Violet, Ruby, Zoe, Connie, and Alicia—got to work right away. Soon the room was alive with the sound of **clicking** keyboards and excited squeaking as the rodents made COMMENTS and **suggestions** on the articles.

After a few hours, the sky had turned a deep **BLUE**. The issue was finally ready.

"Mouselets, we did it!" Tanja cheered.

"Let's celebrate with a few *cups* of cocoa," Violet said. "I'll go put the kettle on."

Outside the office, something caught her attention. Two **envelopes** were sticking out of a suggestion box the newspaper staff had placed there for letters and comments from the academy's students.

"Someone wrote to the **paper**," Violet exclaimed as she came back into the room

with the envelopes in her paw. Real
letters were rare, since most readers sent
e-mails with their comments. In fact,
the mouselets scarcely paid any attention to
the suggestion box.

"Let's read them **RIGHT AWAY**," Colette
suggested. "Maybe we'll get some inspiration
for our next issue."

Nicky opened the **pink** envelope and removed a piece of paper.

"A mouselet is asking for advice about her summer **vacation**," she summed up as she scanned the letter. "Maybe we should do an article about vacation **DESTINATIONS**."

What are the letters about?

Listen to this!

Pam chose the **YELLOW** envelope. "Listen to this! A rat named Carl is asking us to publish our favorite **pizza** recipe. What a **scrumptious** subject!"

"From one pizza lover to another," Paulina joked. "Sounds like the perfect topic for you, Pam."

While the mouselets were **GiGGLiNG**, Tanja spotted an envelope under her chair. "Hey, here's another one!" She picked it up, tore open the envelope, and began reading.

"Hey, Tanja, is everything okay?" Colette asked. "Your snout just turned **redder** than Pam's favorite tomato sauce!"

Tanja smiled shyly. "You'll never believe it, mouselets," she explained. "Someone here at the academy has a **secret admirer!**"

What a romantic letter!

THIS IS TRUE ROMANCE!

At Tanja's words, the mouselets all started squeaking at once.

"A **secret admirer**?"

"Can you tell who *wrote* the letter?"

"Who is it **FOR**?"

"Let me **SEE**!"

"Let me **read** it, too!"

Curious as a pack of cats, the editorial team huddled around Tanja. They were all dying to read the **mysterious** letter. As the paper was passed from paw to paw, a dreamy silence fell over the room.

Colette was the first to break the silence. "No doubt about it—this is **true** romance!"

My dearest cheese niblet,

You don't know how much I adore you. I wish I could find the right words to tell you how much I admire you when we're in class together, or as you scurry across campus.

I wrote this poem to tell you how I feel, though I'll never find the courage to give it to you!

Shall I compare thee to a slice of cheese?
Thou art lovelier than flavors like these.
Brie is a treat, but you are sweeter.
Swiss is bliss, but you are neater!
So long as mice can squeak or eyes can see,
I'll be your friend and devote myself to thee.

Ruby stood up and snatched the letter. "Of course it is. Stop sticking your snout in my **personal business**!"

Ruby was the most popular mouselet at the academy. She was always surrounded by a gaggle of **admirers**, and she was sure that the letter was meant for her.

"I don't see your name on the envelope, Ruby," Nicky pointed out, **TURNING** it over in her paws.

"Right," Tanja said, gently pulling the paper away from Ruby. "And your name isn't on the letter, either."

"It's obviously meant for **ME**!" Ruby protested. "Who else would it be for?"

"Actually, we don't even know if it's for a boy or a girl mouse! This could be intended for any **rodent** on campus," Pam argued. "Think about it: a mouse who's

too **shy** to proclaim his or her feelings writes an anonymouse letter and sends it to the school **NEWSPAPER** to have it published . . ."

Violet nodded. "Pam's right! This way, the mouse he—or she—is crushing on could read his or her *words*," Violet concluded. "And the writer wouldn't have to reveal his or her identity."

"**It's so romantic!**" Colette sighed. "What a sweet, sincere letter. Too bad the author doesn't have the **COURAGE** to come forward."

"So let's help this mouse declare him or herself," said Nicky. "Let's **publish** the letter in the newspaper and ask the mystery mouse to reveal his or her identity!"

Everyone liked the idea, but there was one problem: The latest issue of the newspaper was already closed, and it was too **LATE** to add another article.

Tanja quickly came up with a solution: They could post the letter on the newspaper's **blog**, which all the students on campus read daily.

And so, on that same evening, Paulina posted the letter online, inviting the **mysterious** letter writer to reveal his or her identity.

The search for the **secret admirer** had begun!

THE MYSTERY OF ANONYMOUSE

The next morning, practically every rodent on campus was buzzing about the anonymouse letter. There were dozens of funny and FASCINATING comments posted on the newspaper's blog. *The Case of the Secret Crush,* as the students called it, was the most intriguing thing to happen at Mouseford Academy since the cafeteria had started serving fat-free cheese!

Ruby didn't miss an opportunity to BOAST about her secret admirer. She was sashaying around campus telling everybody that the letter was all about her!

"I insisted on having the letter published," she declared.

"That poor rodent was so sweet to *write* to me that I'm willing to meet him. I'm sure I'll hear from him today."

Pam and Violet exchanged skeptical glances.

"Betcha an extra-cheese **pizza** that letter was not for her," Pam whispered, winking.

The mouselet in the letter is me!

Hmm . . .

Violet nodded. "What do you say we go check the blog? Maybe there's **news**!"

In the computer lab, the two friends met up with Paulina. She was in charge of running the blog and had spent the whole morning in front of the **computer**, hoping the author would reveal his identity.

After a few minutes, Colette and Nicky joined them.

"Nicky, you're here, too?!" Violet said. "What about gymnastics **practice**?"

"And you, Colette?" Pam added. "Aren't you supposed to be doing **research** on Japanese theater for Professor Plotfur?"

"Um . . ." the two friends stuttered, blushing redder than a pair of cheese rinds.

Then they looked at each other and burst out **laughing**. This mystery had struck a chord with every student on campus. The young mice were all obsessed!

Suddenly, Paulina jumped up.

"*There he is!*" she exclaimed. "**It's him!**"

The mouselets gasped and gazed at the computer screen. "What did he **write**?"

"Has he revealed his **identity**?" Colette asked. "Or *her* identity, I mean?"

Paulina shook her snout. "No, nothing like that," she replied. "But there's another **letter**!"

"Rotten rats' teeth! We're dealing with one **MYSTERIOUS** mouse here." Pam sighed.

Colette was already reading the letter. "It's true, but this letter is *SO BEAUTIFUL*, I almost don't mind! You've got to read it, Pam."

"Well, one mystery has been cleared up," Nicky noticed. "This time our mysterious writer has called himself *Romeo*, just like the famouse character in *Romeo and Juliet* by William Squeakspeare! So I'm guessing he's a boy."

My darling cheese nip,

At last my words can reach you, thanks to this blog!

So scrape the cheese out of your ears and listen, my sweet little cheese stick.

If you do, you'll hear my heart beat to the sound of your dance steps, as soft and light as freshly grated Parmesan on pasta.

I am thinking of you.

Yours,
Romeo

A LOVE SONG

In the days that followed, the obsession with the mysterious Romeo spread faster than the smell of baked Brie. Romeo's identity was still a secret, but every day a new **ROMANTIC** message was posted on the blog. After a week, Romeo's fans formed a club in his honor.

"Look what Elly gave me," Nicky said one morning, catching up with her friends outside the music room. "This is the latest fashion from the Romeo Club. Cute, isn't it?"

She showed the Thea Sisters a funny green T-shirt with glittery writing on it. "Oh, Romeo, Romeo, who art thou, Romeo?"

"Does it come in **PINK**, too?" Colette asked eagerly.

"Wait, did you join the Romeo Club, Nicky?" Craig said as he and Shen scampered up to the girls.

The mouselets *giggled*.

"No, we're not in the club," Pam assured him.

"Good!" Craig replied. "Then you might want to join my new group." He opened his jacket to reveal a white T-shirt with big letters that read: **I am not Romeo!**

Just then Professor Aria called the students into the **classroom**. "Hurry up, slowpokes, class is starting! Come on in!"

The mouselets **rushed** to their seats. This was certainly not the time to try to uncover Romeo's identity.

But there was someone who just couldn't

stop brooding about it: Ruby. She was still trying to convince everyone she was the object of Romeo's affection, but the days kept slipping by and he still hadn't come forward. Some of her classmates had even started teasing her about it!

"This is getting more unbearable than the final season of **Mouse Idol**!" Ruby whispered to Connie as Professor Aria began her lecture. "Today there was another letter, but that CHEESEBRAIN Romeo still hasn't revealed himself! What is he waiting for? A balcony? A personal invitation?"

"But they're such nice letters!" said Alicia, who was sitting behind her. "I printed them out so I can carry them with me all the time."

As she squeaked, she tried to pass the bundle of letters to her friend, but the rubber band holding them together

broke and the letters cascaded to the floor. Alicia gasped in embarrassment.

Professor Aria took one look at the papers **strewn** across the floor and said, "What's this? Has Romeo started delivering his letters straight to our classroom?"

Her students all sat up straight, expecting a scolding, but the professor had something else in mind. She smiled at them mischievously.

"Class, for a week now we've been talking nonstop about *love*, am I right?" she asked.

Her reply came from a mouselet sitting in the first row, who let out a long **sigh**.

"So here's what we'll do," the professor continued. "Our next assignment will be **musical**! By the end of next week, I want each of you to write a **love song**."

THE CLUES
DON'T ADD UP!

"Professor Aria is really a MOUSERIFIC teacher," Pam said as they scurried out of class. "She always comes up with interesting **incentives** for us to do our homework."

"Yeah, it's true," Nicky agreed. "If only this assignment would give Romeo some incentive to reveal his *identity*!"

"You said it, sis," Paulina said. "We were hoping to help make his romance a reality, but Romeo seems determined to avoid the spotlight."

Colette looked **pensive**. "What do you say we give him a little help? **Come with me!**" She led the mouselets up to her room.

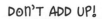

"We don't have many clues to Romeo's identity," Colette explained as she stretched out on her bed with printouts of Romeo's letters. "But we have a lot of clues to help us figure out who the object of his affection is!"

Grinning, she picked up one of Romeo's letters. But before she could continue, Nicky interjected, "Don't squeak, Coco. I know who the real JULIET is!"

Let's follow the clues!

The mouselets' jaws all dropped open.

Nicky nodded. "Listen to this and tell me if it reminds you of anyone." She began reciting one of the letters from memory:

25

"'My darling furface, you devote yourself to sports. You are as graceful as a guinea pig, as fast as a hamster on a wheel, as limber as a lemur . . .'"

There could be no **doubt** about it: that description fit Nicky perfectly! So was *Nicky* the mysterious Juliet?

"Okay, but what do you say about this?" Violet interrupted, pulling a **PieCe oF PaPeR** from her pocket. "'Your paws touch your instrument's strings as lightly as the wings of a butterfly. The notes you spin are as smooth as cream cheese on a bagel, as melodic as Muenster sizzling on a griddle, as gorgeous as goat cheese topped with Gorgonzola . . .'"

"Curdled cottage cheese!" Paulina exlaimed. "That sounds like you, Vi! The letters must be about you . . ."

"Wait a minute!" Pam interrupted her. "Have you forgotten that letter he wrote about a rodent with soft, CURLY fur who loves pepperoni pizza?"

"But it doesn't make any sense!" blurted Colette, who had not said a word until then. "Here Romeo writes about fur that shines like Swiss cheese in the sun . . . he must be writing about a blonde!"

The mouselets were squeakless. Each one recognized herself in PASSAGES of some letters. What could it mean?

When the mouselets compared the various descriptions in the letters, though, something didn't add up.

"You would almost think that all of us are Juliet!" Pam exclaimed.

"So that means none of us is," Paulina concluded.

For a moment, there was a look of **disappointment** on each mouselet's snout. But their sad expressions were quickly replaced by **laughter**.

"Still, it really did sound like he was writing about us!" Violet said, once the giggling had died down.

"Uh-huh," Nicky **REMARKED**. "Somewhere out there is a mouselet who's a mix of all five of us put together!"

"Yeah," Pam said. "I have no idea who it could be, but whoever she is, I already **like** her!"

I AM JULIET!

In the meantime, on the other side of the academy, Ruby was **gearing up** to prove she was Juliet. Romeo was writing to her—she had no **doubt**!

"Are you sure?" Alicia asked **innocently**, scrolling through the blog on Ruby's computer. "Here it says: '. . . your dance steps, as soft and light as freshly grated Parmesan . . .'"

"What are you saying? You think I'm a bad **dancer**?" Ruby replied, annoyed.

"Oh, we all know you're a great dancer, Ruby," Connie quickly put in. "But how do you explain this? He writes: 'I love listening to you while you play . . .'"

Ruby **GLARED** at her. "Just what are

you implying, Connie?" she hissed. "I play the **ViOLiN** perfectly well. It's just that . . . um . . . I don't have much time to practice!"

"Maybe," Zoe said. "But I've never seen you hit the *gym*, and listen to this: 'My darling furface, you devote yourself to sports. You are as graceful as a guinea pig, as fast as a hamster on a wheel, as limber as a lemur . . .'"

Alicia, Connie, and Zoe all burst out **laughing**, making Ruby fly to her paws in fury. "**THaT'S iT!** I've had enough of you three. Go on, skedaddle!" she shouted. "Do you want to

I will prove it's me!

know where I'm going now? Well, do you?"

The rest of the Ruby Crew stopped at the door, intrigued.

"I'm going for a *jog*!" Ruby exclaimed before slamming the door in their snouts.

Like the Thea Sisters, Ruby had **carefully** studied Romeo's letters. But she refused to accept that she was not the mouselet described in them!

Romeo praises his Juliet's athletic ability? Ruby takes up running!

Romeo's crush likes music? Ruby tries the violin!

Over the next few days, Ruby worked hard to embody the mouselet described in the letters. Sadly, the results were not as **brilliant** as she'd hoped. Soon Ruby realized she was no good at SPORTS, had no idea how to play a musical instrument, and didn't even know how to FRY an egg.

Finally, after getting the best furdresser

Juliet loves cooking . . . but for Ruby it's a true mystery!

Naturally curly fur does not come naturally to Ruby!

on Whale Island to transform her long, straight locks into soft, **curly** fur, she gave up. There was nothing left to do but reach out to the only rodent who could help her.

THE FIRST CLUE

Ruby headed straight toward the academy's rehearsal hall and **barged** into the room where Ryder was working on his song for Professor Aria.

"Hey!" he complained, annoyed by his sister's rude behavior. "Haven't you ever heard of knocking?"

Ruby SMILED. "Oh dearest little brother, everyone says you are a real musical genius, a natural talent . . ."

Ryder looked at her SUSPICIOUSLY. Ruby never said anything nice about him unless she wanted something!

"Okay, sis, what do you want?" he said cautiously.

Ruby giggled. "Well, to begin with, could

Dearest little brother . . .

What?

you teach me how to play *guitar*? I have to learn quickly. I mean really quickly. Like right **NOW**!"

Ryder shook his snout. "Oh, I get it. Now you're going to tell me Romeo has nothing to do with your sudden interest in **music**, right?"

"Wh-what?" Ruby stuttered, trying to look surprised. "Of course not! It's just that . . . well, you know, I've always been very *fond* of music."

"Ruby, you're hopeless!" said Ryder, rolling his eyes.

"Turning yourself into someone you're not won't do you any good. You'll just end up **_disappointed_**."

"Want to bet?" Ruby cried. "I'll wager you that soon the *famouse* Romeo will be putty in my paws."

Ryder laughed. But his sister was as serious as a seven-cheese pizza!

"Fine, *challenge* accepted," he said.

Ruby smiled with satisfaction and scampered away.

Ryder just shook his snout again. "You're really going to make a **MESS** of things, Ruby . . ."

Down the hall, the Thea Sisters were in another **rehearsal** room. There were just a few more days before Professor Aria's homework assignment was due, and the mouselets still had a lot of work to do.

The melody was ready, but the words were a problem.

"I wish Romeo were here. He would know what to write! If only we knew who he is . . ." Violet mumbled.

"Anybody could have put that letter in the suggestion **BOX**," Paulina remarked.

When Nicky heard those words, something clicked. "Wait a minute. What if Romeo **didn't** put that letter in the box?"

The other mouselets turned to look at her, puzzled.

"Think about it," Nicky went on. "There were only two *letters* on the table: I read one, and Pam read the other!"

Violet opened her eyes wide. "You're right! The letter about **vacation spots** and the one about *pizza* . . ."

"And then Tanja found the other letter

under her chair . . ." Paulina said slowly. "Someone must have left it behind in the newsroom! It was probably one of the eight rodents working on the sports **section**. When Tanja found it, we assumed it came from the **suggestion box**!"

The Thea Sisters rejoiced: they had finally discovered a clue to the mysterious mouse's **identity**!

"Can you believe it?" Colette said. "Romeo is one of our *friends*!"

"It could be **Craig**," Nicky guessed.

"Impossible," Violet replied. "He's president of the 'I Am Not Romeo' club!"

"Then it could be 𝖲𝖧𝖤𝖭 . . ." Pam said.

"Or **Ryder**!"

"Why not 𝕾𝖊𝖇𝖆𝖘𝖙𝖎𝖆𝖓?"

Paulina had remained quiet as a mouse as her friends speculated. Suddenly, she lit up. "Mouselets, I have an idea! We can have our cheese and eat it, too. I have the perfect idea how to solve our lyrics problem *and* the Romeo mystery. We just have to wait for the day of Professor Aria's *assignment* . . ."

DON'T OVERDO IT, RUBY!

The next day, Nicky woke up early for her usual **morning run**. On her way back to campus, she noticed a mouselet working out on the grass by the academy's entrance.

"Hey, Tanja!" she said. "You're already UP, too?"

Her friend grinned at her. "I just made it onto the **gymnastics** team, so I try to work out every day."

The two rodents walked back to the dorm together, and after a SHOWER, they scurried toward their first class of the day:

Professor Plié's dance lesson.

Inside the practice room, they took places at the barre near the other Thea Sisters.

"Just think about it," Colette was saying as she slid into her BALLET SLIPPERS. "Romeo is probably here right now, LOOKING for his Juliet . . ."

"What a lucky mouselet!" Tanja sighed. "Ever since we found the first letter, I've done nothing but dream about it. It's so romantic, don't you think?"

The Thea Sisters agreed, and Paulina quickly shared their theory with Tanja.

"Would you like to help us with our

***investigation*?**" Pam asked.

"That would be nice," she replied. "But today I promised Ruby I'd stop by her first guitar lesson to **listen to her play**."

"Ruby is learning to play an **instrument**?!" Colette exclaimed, surprised.

"Yep," Tanja said. "I was surprised, too, but she seems really interested."

Professor Plié called the class to order, and the dance lesson began.

Bravo!

After the warm-up, the students lined up single file. One at a time, they tried a few JUMPS under their professor's watchful eye.

At the back of the room, Ruby **whispered** to a small group of mouselets.

"I'm sure it's my dance skills that attracted Romeo," she boasted. "After all, I am the best in this class—"

A chorus of cheers interrupted her. Ruby turned around, curious.

Tanja had just performed a difficult jump with a **split**, and her classmates were so impressed they had spontaneously started applauding.

Everyone was gazing at Tanja in admiration. Even Professor Plié came over to CONGRATULATE her.

"Moldy mozzarella!" Ruby hissed. "Romeo could be here right now. I can't let anyone steal the **spotlight**!"

So she elbowed her way to the front of the **line** and got ready for her jump.

Check out my moves, Romeo! Ruby thought as she began **running**.

Unfortunately, she pushed off too hard, and her momentum carried her too high. Ruby executed a **spectacular** midair split, but she couldn't stick the landing!

Ouchie!

She howled like a wounded wombat as she belly flopped onto the **polished** parquet dance floor.

Tanja was the first to reach her side. A moment later, the rest of Ruby's classmates

had surrounded them. Tanja took Ruby's paws and PULLED her up.

Thankfully, Ruby was not **badly** hurt, but Professor Plié asked Tanja to take her to the **nurse** anyway. That was the end of the dance class for the day.

iT'S ELEMENTARY, SiSTERS!

After Ruby's belly flop, the Thea Sisters headed toward the locker room.

"Why does Ruby always have to *overdo* it?" asked Pam, shaking her snout.

"Maybe she thought Romeo was there to **watch her**," Violet speculated. "You know she's convinced he's writing about her."

Her friends were **QUIET**, but they were all thinking the same thing: Certainly Romeo, who seemed to be a *sincere* and **straightforward** mouse, wouldn't be impressed by a stunt like Ruby's!

"Did you see Tanja's jump?" Paulina exclaimed. "She's really **talented**!"

Colette stopped **COMBING** her long blonde

fur. "'Your dance steps are as light and agile as a gerbil's . . .'" she recited. "What a funny coincidence."

"Wait a minute, wait a minute!" Pam cried. "By cheese, I think I've got it! Remember the letter I thought was about me? Well, you know who else has curly fur and loves pizza?"

The mouselets looked at one another. They were all thinking the same thing.

"'Your paws touch your instrument's strings as lightly as the wings of a butterfly,'" Violet quoted.

"Of course!" Nicky exclaimed. "Tanja knows how to play guitar! And this morning I ran into her while she was working out: She's on the gymnastics team, too!"

Paulina nodded and quoted another

sentence from Romeo's **letter**: "'You are as graceful as a guinea pig, as fast as a hamster on a wheel, as limber as a lemur . . .'"

How could the Thea Sisters have missed it? The mouselet they were looking for was their good friend **Tanja**!

But of course . . . it has to be her!

A RELUCTANT ROMEO

The Thea Sisters had figured out who the anonymouse letters were written for. Meanwhile, someone else was sure she'd figured out who the mysterious secret admirer was!

Zoe had had a crush on Ryder forever, and over the last few days, she'd become more and more convinced that *Ryder was Romeo*. After all, he'd even played Romeo in the school play!* And the more she thought about it, the more certain she became that she was the LUCKY Juliet.

Zoe gazed at Ryder during lectures and started trailing him between classes. Then one morning she saw him in the *hallway*

---

*To get the full story, check out the book *Drama at Mouseford*.

and decided that it was time to come forward.

"Ryder, stop pretending!" she exclaimed. "I know you're the one who writes those **beautiful** letters for me! Don't hide from me, my Romeo!"

She **dashed** toward Ryder with her paws wide open. When he realized what was happening, he started **running away**! Zoe followed right on his tail.

When Ryder reached the rehearsal halls, he opened the first available door, breathless, and stepped into the Thea Sisters' practice room.

"Don't say a word, please!" he begged them. "I'm running away!"

The mouselets stopped rehearsing their song and turned to stare at him.

"I'm sorry to interrupt," he said hastily. "It's just that Zoe has decided she's JULiet, and she thinks I'm her Romeo! Ridiculous, right?"

The Thea Sisters didn't reply, but they did exchange a **meaningful** look. Ryder was a member of the sports staff, and he was also very sensitive and romantic, even though he tried his best to hide it.

"Mouselets?" he went on, *worried*. "You don't think it's me, do you? Come on, what do I have to do to convince you I'm not Romeo? Look, I'm even wearing one of those funny **T-shirts**!"

He opened his jacket, and the mouselets immediately recognized the writing:

The Thea Sisters burst out *laughing*. He'd convinced them at last!

Just then they heard Zoe's shrill squeak outside the room. "My Romeo, where are you hiding? Come on, don't be shy!"

Ryder shushed them, begging for silence. A moment later, they heard Zoe's pawsteps as she scurried away.

Ryder breathed a sigh of relief. "I just hope Romeo hurries up and reveals himself! I can't take it anymore!"

"What do you think? Should we tell him?" Paulina asked her friends.

"Tell him?" Ryder asked. "Tell me what?"

Violet quickly **summarized** their THEORY: Juliet's identity, the plan to figure out who Romeo was, and the hint that it was one of the ratlets who worked on the *sports* page.

"Tanja doesn't know anything about this yet," Pam explained. "We don't want to be the ones to reveal Romeo's 𝖲𝖤𝖢𝖱𝖤𝖳. He has to be the one to do it."

Ryder was listening intently, thinking, *I knew all along those letters weren't about Ruby!*

"You know the ratlets of the editorial staff better than we do," Nicky said. "Will you help us?"

Ryder agreed at once. He was more than ready for a *happy ending* to this love story! And he also had an idea for a little prank to play on his sister . . .

RYDER'S
SCHEME

Back in his room, Ryder sat down at his desk and started thinking. He was so tired of his sister's **SELF-ABSORBED** schemes. Maybe he could teach her to be a more thoughtful mouse in the *future*.

He pulled out a sheet of paper and started *writing*. *Flower of my heart, you are more fragrant than feta . . .*

When he finished, he stretched out and *admired* his work: Any rodent worth his cheese would mistake it for an authentic Romeo letter!

That evening, Ryder knocked on his sister's door. The **envelope** with the letter was in his paw.

Ha, ha, ha!

"Oh, it's you!" Ruby said, looking at him suspiciously. Did you come to apologize for being **RUDE** to me?"

Ryder stifled a giggle. "Actually, I'm here because of Romeo . . ."

Ruby's **green** eyes lit up with interest. "Romeo? Come on in, quick!"

"It looks like you're right about the letters,"

Ryder began. "Today I found this in the *math* room . . .

Ruby was gazing at the envelope in Ryder's paw. "A letter . . . from Romeo?" she asked.

"This time he even wrote your *name* on the envelope!" her brother fibbed. "It must be *special*. Otherwise he would

Hooray! A letter from Romeo!

have posted it on the blog like the others. Don't you want to read it?"

Ruby nodded **TRIUMPHANTLY**. "Of course, but first I have to call my crew!"

She grabbed her phone and started calling her *friends*. A few minutes later, Alicia, Connie, and Zoe were on her doorstep in their **pajamas**, half asleep.

"Ryder!" Zoe whispered. "Is it true there's a Romeo letter for Ruby?"

"Uh-huh," he replied. "I told you those letters weren't from me!"

Zoe sighed with disappointment. But inwardly, Ryder was rejoicing: Thanks to the **fake** letter, Zoe would finally leave him alone!

Ruby was very **eXCiteD**. She opened the letter and read it aloud as everybody listened.

Sweet Juliet,

The time has come to meet!

Up until now I did not have the courage, but I can no longer remain silent. I must gaze into your beautiful emerald eyes and tell you the whole truth.

Meet me at Turtle Beach, north of Kneecap River, when the next full moon rises.

I will wait for you.

Romeo

"**Wow,**" Connie commented. "A rendezvous with Romeo!"

"But you can only get to that ***beach*** by boat," Alicia said, *worried*.

"So what's the problem? Reaching it will be a piece of cheesecake!" Ruby replied with a triumphant look.

"But what if Prince Charming turns out to be a *frog*?" Zoe asked.

Ruby had a quick reply ready. "That's why you can't talk about this with anybody. Not until I've met him!"

Ryder was secretly ENJOYING every minute of this conversation. But when he heard those words, his ears pricked up.

"Don't you get it? I don't give a *cheesy chew* about silly Romeo," Ruby explained. "I just want to prove that no one can resist my CHARMS!"

Ryder rolled his eyes: His sister was hopeless! For a minute there, he'd felt bad about tricking her. But now he was sure he was doing the right thing. His sister needed

to learn a lesson! And if no one else was going to teach her, it was up to him. After all, he was her brother.

"If I like him, I might even ask him for an interview," Ruby concluded. "Imagine the scoop: **Ruby reveals the identity of the mysterious Romeo!**"

I'll get a great scoop!

ROMEO'S RAP

On the day Professor Aria's song was due, the Thea Sisters were jumping out of their fur with excitement. They were finally going to discover **WHO** Romeo really was!

Paulina's plan was simple but clever: Pam, Nicky, and Colette had chosen a few *lines* from Romeo's letters and paired them with some **beats** Violet and Paulina had created. The five friends would perform together. Thus, **ROMEO'S RAP** was born!

The Thea Sisters were certain that when Romeo heard his words set to music, he would **react**. The mouselets planned to scan the snouts in the crowd until they spotted him.

"I'm so **nervous** about singing my

song in front of everyone!" Tanja said. She had no **IDEA** what the Thea Sisters were up to.

"Everything's going to be great," Nicky reassured her. "We're all rooting for you!"

Tanja **BLUSHED**. "Thank you, mouselets! You are the best friends a rodent could have."

How exciting!

Are you ready?

"What are you going to sing?" Elly asked the Thea Sisters.

"It's a surprise," Pam replied, smiling.

The performance hall was as crowded as the **Cheddar Chopper** grocery store the day before Thanksgiving. Practically every rodent in the academy wanted to hear the brand-new songs their fellow students were going to perform.

The Thea Sisters joined Professor Aria, who was surrounded by synthesizers, speakers, microphones, and a mountain of tangled wires.

"Hi, mouselets," Professor Aria greeted them. "Can you help me move these desks? We have to make room for the performers."

Violet was NERVOUS. Big audiences always made her feel uncomfortable.

"Come on, Vi," Colette encouraged her.

"Maybe today we'll find out who Romeo is!"

"I just hope we can find him in this crowd," Pam grumbled, setting up the microphones and cables like a real **professional**.

Finally, at ten thirty, Professor Aria began to squeak. "Dear students, last week I gave your classmates a very *difficult* assignment."

The crowded hall was so *quiet*, you could

hear a cheese slice drop. The audience was completely **focused**.

"Today we are all here together to find out how each of these students expresses **love** through music," the professor went on. "So let's show these rodents some love of our own!"

The audience **clapped** their paws enthusiastically, and the performances began. Some of the songs were touching, others poetic, others funny. Everyone had done their best and put a little bit of him or herself into **SONG**.

When it was Tanja's turn, the Thea Sisters leaned in close. Surely Romeo would be the most **alert** rodent in the audience!

Tanja began singing a **sweet melody**, which gathered in strength when it came time for the chorus. Her lyrics were **simple** but

heartfelt. Her song was about spending the
PERFECT DAY with the rodent you liked.

A ratlet with **brown** fur slowly elbowed
his way through the crowd until he stood
right in front of Tanja. Colette noticed
his gaze and gave Nicky's tail a quick tug.
"PSSSST! Look over there!"

"Could he be our Romeo?" Nicky
whispered back.

When you are around, the moon shines brighter!

"We'll find out soon enough," Pam said. "Let's keep an **EYE** on him when it's our turn to perform."

Just then Tanja finished her song to rounds of applause. Now it was the Thea Sisters' turn.

Paulina looked at Ryder, who was standing behind the turntable, and nodded for him to start the music. It was time for **ROMEO'S RAP**!

After a few moments, the audience was swept up in the beat. They started **clapping** in time. Everyone was excited . . . except for the ratlet with brown fur the Thea Sisters had noticed before. In fact, he looked shocked. He must've recognized his own words in the rap, and he began **blushing** redder than a cheese rind.

But he soon regained control of himself.

He looked around, ears drooping with embarrassment, and then **scampered away**!

B-but . . .

Romeo's Rap ended in a standing ovation, but the mouselets were already thinking about a *different* kind of success.

The Thea Sisters gave Ryder a knowing nod, and he grinned back at them. He had seen everything, and there was no doubt in his mind: The ratlet with the brown fur was the mysterious

Romeo!

THE MISSING NOTEBOOK

After their triumphant performance, the mouselets had to split up to go to their **respective** classes. But at three o'clock on the dot, they were back together for an afternoon snack in the cafeteria, and Ryder soon joined them. Only Nicky was missing, since she was busy with gymnastics practice.

"Romeo's real name is Ron," Ryder told the mouselets. "He just started going to Mouseford, but he's cool. He's already made a lot of friends."

"He takes the same *photography class* I do," Paulina said. "He's really nice!"

"Yeah, he's a good photographer. That's

why we signed him up for the paper's SPORTS staff," Ryder said.

Now that they knew who Romeo was, all that was left was to get him to REVEAL himself. Unlike Ruby, the Thea Sisters weren't interested in a big SCOOP. They just wanted Tanja and Ron to *meet*, not to put either of them in the spotlight! But how? The mouselets racked their brains for a solution.

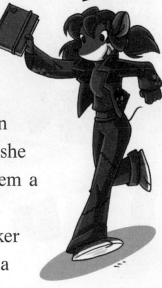

Look here!

Just then Nicky walked in with an enourmouse SMILE on her snout. "Look here!" she said happily, showing them a red NOTEBOOK.

"I found this in the locker room, and it gave me a

great idea! Here's the plan . . ."

During practice, Tanja had **forgotten** one of her notebooks in the locker room. Nicky found it, and she had a **brilliant** idea for how to use it.

The next day, Ryder put Nicky's plan into action. At the beginning of photography class, he approached Ron and asked him to do an **interview** for the sports section.

"But I've never done an interview before!" the ratlet protested. "I'm a photographer, not a writer, remember?"

"It'll be **REALLY EASY**, trust me!" Ryder said. "You just have to talk to Nicky, our gymnastics star. She's super **friendly**, you'll see."

Ron was not persuaded, so Ryder went on. "All the editors are busy, and no one else can do it. Plus, this is a good opportunity to get your name out there!" Without waiting for Ron to reply, Ryder **quickly** said, "Nicky will be in the gym tonight at six o'clock. You're a real pal — thanks!"

Ron had no choice but to accept the

Thanks, Ron!

job. Ryder left, **pleased** as a porcupine. The first part of Nicky's plan had worked!

In the meantime, the Thea Sisters were getting ready for stage two. At the end of the interview, Nicky would leave Tanja's notebook behind. She would leave it out for Ron to see. The Thea Sisters were sure Tanja's **secret admirer** wouldn't be able to resist the chance to write one of his famous *letters* in it.

And that's when the mouselets would spring into action! They would find Tanja and make up an excuse to take her to the GYM just as Ron was writing in her notebook! Caught in the act, Ron/Romeo would have no choice but to reveal himself.

"And love will take care of the rest!" Colette declared.

A DANGEROUS
TURN OF EVENTS

Timing was crucial for the Thea Sisters' plan to work. The mouselets were pretty much ready for any surprise . . . or at least they thought they were!

While Nicky was sitting down in front of the *microphone*, getting ready for Ron's interview, Ruby was about to embark on a **very dangerous** kayak trip.

"Getting all the way out there will be hard," she told the rest of the Ruby Crew. "But tonight there is a full moon, and my **RoMeo exposé** is waiting for me at Turtle Beach."

She began rowing as the sun was setting.

"Ruby is so **brave**," Zoe said admiringly.

"She'd face any danger to get a scoop."

Ryder was missing, too. He was in a hurry to get to **Turtle Beach** before his sister!

Meanwhile Ron's interview with Nicky was coming to an end. It had been a very pleasant **conversation**. Nicky was pleased to discover that Tanja's admirer was so **friendly** and *funny*!

As planned, when they said good-bye,

Nicky left Tanja's notebook behind.

Romeo is ready, she thought as she headed toward the locker room. *Now it's up to the mouselets; let's hope they get* Juliet *here in time!*

Colette, Pam, Paulina, and Violet were wandering all over Mouseford Academy,

Good-bye!

looking for Tanja. They couldn't seem to track her down. But they did run into the **Ruby Crew**.

"Hey there," said Violet. "Have you seen Tanja anywhere?"

"No," said Zoe. "But let me give you a *little advice*." She couldn't wait to tell everyone about Ruby's big **Scoop**.

"No, let me," Connie interrupted. "Don't bother wasting any more time trying to figure out who Romeo is. Ruby's **beat** you to it this time!"

The Thea Sisters looked at one another, confused. What were Connie and Zoe squeaking about?

"What do you mean, Connie?" asked Colette.

Connie and Zoe refused to say another word. But Alicia was **WORRIED** about

Ruby's reckless outing, so she spilled the cheese about the mysterious **rendezvous**.

"I can't believe this!" Pam exclaimed.

"You can't believe what?" asked Nicky, who was just joining her friends.

Violet quickly filled her in.

"Alicia's whole story is stranger than cream cheese on a pickle," said Paulina. "There's no way the real Romeo set up that rendezvous. Because we know he's crushing on Tanja!"

Weird...

"That's not what worries me right now," Nicky put in. "I know Turtle Beach really well: You can only reach it by river, and the undertow is very tricky. Whoever sent her down there is playing a **dangerous** prank!"

Pam frowned. "When Ruby left, it was

still daylight, but now it's completely **dark**! How will she avoid the rocks and whirlpools on the way back?"

Violet looked worried. "Guys, let's forget about Tanja and Ron for a minute. We've got a more IMPORTANT mission."

Colette nodded. "Ruby is in danger. We need to **do** something!"

As the Thea Sisters were rushing to plan a rescue mission, Ruby had finally reached the rendezvous spot. The sand was sparkling in the light of the moon. Normally, Ruby would have been squeakless at such a beautiful sight, but right now her mood was anything but ROMANTIC.

After rowing through miles of rapids, with thorny bushes on the water's edge tearing at her fur and water splashing in her snout, she was exhausted!

But who . . .?

"Well, have you enjoyed your little adventure?" came a squeak from behind her. "Now will you stop trying to make yourself into **someone you're not**?"

Ruby immediately recognized that squeak. She turned around and . . .

A JOKE GONE
TOO FAR

"Ryder!" she shrieked. "What are you doing here?! Did you *follow* me?"

"Yep, I played a little joke on you," he answered, chuckling. "It looks like I'm the winner of our bet!"

Yeah, it's me!

"That letter . . ." the mouselet hissed, getting **angrier** and **angrier**. "You wrote it!"

"I did it for YOU, sis," Ryder tried to explain.

But Ruby wasn't listening to him. "You had me row all this way . . ."

"I did it to **teach** you

a *lesson*," Ryder said. "You need to stop sticking your snout into other rodents' business. You don't always have to be the **center** of attention. Just be yourself, and rodents will like you for who you really are."

Ruby was furious with her brother.

"And I **broke** a pawnail, too!" she cried, **tears** in her eyes. "You are a rotten rodent, and I hope I never see you ever again!"

Ryder tried to stop her, but Ruby was madder than a cat with a bad case of fleas. She **ran** to the kayak, pushing it into the current without another thought.

Ryder realized he'd **gone too far**. He followed his sister into the water. "Come on, Ruby, it was just a **joke**! Come back! I came here to meet you to make sure you'd get back safe and sound!" He pushed his kayak into the river and **followed** his sister.

Unfortunately, the current had grown stronger. And Ruby was **worn out** from her long trip. Plus, she was too upset to pay attention to her paddling. The kayak was tossed left and right by the current. After a few minutes, it was ꮪwirling adrift—and heading away from Mouseford Academy!

The full moon disappeared behind a cloud,

and the night grew even darker. Just then Ruby's kayak **hit** a rock, and she lost her oars.

The kayak toppled over, and Ruby fell into the river!

"**Helppp!**" she screamed, clinging to a nearby rock.

Her brother paddled toward her frantically. He **GRABBED** her by the paw, trying to pull her into his boat.

Ruby was **freezing** and **SOAKED** to the fur. She reached for the slippery side of the kayak but missed and splashed into the rushing current again, **dragging** her brother with her!

RUSHING TO THE RESCUE

Luckily, the Thea Sisters hadn't wasted any **time**. They were already rushing to Ruby's rescue.

Professor Van Kraken had lent the mouselets his **motorboat**, and Pam had steered it to Turtle Beach at top speed. She turned on the boat's **SPOTLIGHT** to help her navigate in the dark.

As they headed into the river's most **treacherous** stretches, Pam slowed down. Suddenly, the mouselets heard calls for help from Ruby and Ryder.

"Ryder is with her?!" Paulina exclaimed, surprised. "Do you think he pulled this prank on his sister?"

"If this was all his lousy idea, he's going to get an **earful** from me," Nicky said. "But first let's pull them out!"

Pam drew the boat as close to Ryder and Ruby as possible. Fortunately, the brother and sister already had *life jackets* on. Colette and Nicky threw the mice two **ropes**. Ruby and Ryder were completely spent, but they managed to grab on.

Colette and Nicky hauled them on board while Violet and Paulina shone flashlights on the water to illuminate the hidden rocks. The rescue took real *teamwork*!

As soon as the two rodents were aboard, Pam turned the boat around and headed back to the academy.

The journey home was completely silent. Ruby was still SCARED and furious with her brother for pulling such a mean prank.

Even the Thea Sisters
were looking at him
sternly. This time Ryder
had gone **too far**!

Grrr!

RUBY, IS THAT REALLY YOU?

Back at the academy, Ryder went to his room to change into dry clothes. Meanwhile, the Thea Sisters took good care of Ruby, who kept SNEEZING. Violet prepared a cup of warm jasmine tea. Nicky and Pam helped Ruby change clothes, and Colette soothed her by gently combing her tangled fur. Paulina treated two scratches Ruby had on her paws. Together they tried to help Ruby relax after her *terrifying adventure*.

"I guess I was wrong about Romeo," Ruby finally admitted, sounding unusually *humble*. "He wasn't writing to me."

The mouselets looked at one another, shocked. "Are we sure we fished the real

Ruby out of that river?" Pam whispered to Nicky.

Colette felt sorry for Ruby and tried to comfort her. "It's true you were wrong about Romeo. But, Ruby, you have lots of good QUALITIES. You don't need to imitate other rodents to be popular!"

For a moment, Ruby was **touched**. But she recovered quickly, and soon she'd regained her usual arrogance. "Of course I don't!" she exclaimed. "I am a Flashyfur; it's other rodents who imitate *me*!"

The Thea Sisters **smiled**. The real Ruby was back!

There was a **tentative** knock at the door.

"Hi, uh, can I come in?" Ryder asked. "Ruby, I owe you an APOLOGY."

Ruby was still angry. She glared at her

brother. As for the Thea Sisters, they were shocked that Ryder had put his sister in such a **dangerous** predicament. But they let the brother and sister squeak privately. They could tell from the look on his snout that Ryder felt really *sorry*.

He apologized **sincerely**, and his sister eventually forgave him.

Once the brother and sister were on

squeaking terms again, Violet remembered their plan to figure out *Romeo's* identity. She quickly filled Ruby and Ryder in.

Ruby **glared** at her brother again. "So there's another thing you totally moused up, Ryder. Because of you, the Thea Sisters' plan went up in smoke, and Romeo has yet to find his Juliet!"

Colette, Nicky, Pam, Paulina, and Violet sighed. Now they had to start over from scratch!

A SECRET ALREADY REVEALED

After a good night's sleep, the Thea Sisters woke up rested and full of energy. The previous night's adventure seemed far away, and their attention was back on Romeo and his Juliet.

Pam was a rodent with a plan. "We have to fix things between those two!" she told the other **mouselets** as they were eating breakfast. "If Ron likes Tanja, we should help him find the courage to come forward. No secrets, no tricks—just the plain and **simple** truth!"

Let's help Ron find the courage!

"Well said," Nicky agreed.

"Let's go find Ron and try to persuade him," Paulina said.

DETERMINED to help, the mouselets headed out to find Ron. But as soon as they stepped into the hallway, they met Ruby and her loyal crew.

"Here you are at last," Alicia said.

"You just missed the revelation of the year!" Zoe said. "Romeo is Ron, a ratlet who just started going to Mouseford. Isn't it unbelievable?"

The Thea Sisters were squeakless. How had the Ruby Crew uncovered Ron's secret?

The first suspect, of course, was Ruby, but she just shrugged. "Don't look at me. Everybody already knew about it."

"Except for you mice!" Connie teased. She

tossed her fur and left, *giggling* with her friends.

The Thea Sisters weren't convinced by Ruby's story, but then they ran into Elly, and she also knew Ron's **secret**. And she knew more, too! She knew that Ron's Juliet was Tanja!

Tanja told me!

Ruby was right: Everyone at the academy knew the **truth**. But how had they found out?

Colette asked Elly.

"Well, Tanja told me. How else would I know?" Elly replied. "That mystery was too much for me to **figure** out!"

Just then Craig and Shen passed by on their bikes. When they stopped to say hello, the Thea Sisters noticed Craig was wearing a new T-shirt: **Romeo = Ron**.

"Oh, come on!" Pam snapped. "How did everyone suddenly **guess** the truth?"

"We didn't have to guess," Shen said, **POINTING** across the quad. "Those two told us the truth!"

The Thea Sisters followed Shen's gaze and

saw a couple walking paw in paw. It was Tanja and Ron, together at last!

They told us . . .

ROMEO'S COURAGE

"Well, yes, I'm Romeo!" Ron confessed after he and Tanja joined the mouselets. "You didn't have a *clue*, did you?"

"Well . . ." Pam started, but Violet *gently* touched her paw to stop her.

Hello!

"No, we never guessed!" Violet said quickly.

Pam understood right away: Why *disappoint* him? All's well that ends well, even without the Thea Sisters' help!

"I have to thank Nicky for helping me find the *courage* to come forward," Ron

explained. "Everything changed after our interview."

Colette, Pam, Paulina, and Violet looked at Nicky in surprise, but she looked just as **CONFUSED** as they were!

"Why don't you start from the **beginning** and tell us the entire story?" Pam asked.

"Well, when I realized Nicky's missing **notebook** was really Tanja's, my first thought was to write a *letter* in it. So I started *writing*, but then I changed my mind. I remembered something you'd said during our **INTERVIEW**, Nicky."

Ron continued. "'In sports, there are no shortcuts. Getting out there with no secrets and no tricks is the only way to discover your own limitations. Find a way to overcome those limitations, and you'll succeed.'"

Nicky blushed. She felt a little self-

conscious hearing her words repeated back to her.

The other Thea Sisters **grinned** and rallied around their friend.

"See how wise you are, Nick?" said Paulina proudly.

"Love is like **sports**," Ron went on. "It was time to let Tanja know me for who I really am, with no **PRetending**!"

"So he came to return my notebook," Tanja concluded. "And this time he read his letter to me in the fur, standing right in front of me."

The Thea Sisters were **thrilled**. Ultimately, that was the only real answer: find the courage inside yourself, with no secrets and no tricks!

Just then Ryder and Ruby **joined them**.

"Hey, pal!" Ryder said to Ron. "I just heard the news: **Congratulations!**"

"It's a shame the secret's out, though," Ruby remarked. "I'll miss Romeo's **letters**. They were so romantic . . ."

It was time to let Tanja know me for who I really am.

"Romeo's story doesn't have to end like this," Colette said. "After all, when it comes to **LOVE**, every one of us could be Romeo!"

"You're a genius, Coco!" Paulina exclaimed.

"Let's keep the blog running. We can post stories, poems, and love letters from all the ROMEOS and **Juliets** at Mouseford Academy!"

Don't miss any of these exciting Thea Sisters adventures!

Thea Stilton and the Dragon's Code

Thea Stilton and the Mountain of Fire

Thea Stilton and the Ghost of the Shipwreck

Thea Stilton and the Secret City

Thea Stilton and the Mystery in Paris

Thea Stilton and the Cherry Blossom Adventure

Thea Stilton and the Star Castaways

Thea Stilton: Big Trouble in the Big Apple

Thea Stilton and the Ice Treasure

Thea Stilton and the Secret of the Old Castle

Thea Stilton and the Blue Scarab Hunt

Thea Stilton and the Prince's Emerald

Thea Stilton and the Mystery on the Orient Express

Thea Stilton and the Dancing Shadows

Thea Stilton and the Legend of the Fire Flowers

Thea Stilton and the Spanish Dance Mission

Thea Stilton and the Journey to the Lion's Den

Thea Stilton and the Great Tulip Heist

Thea Stilton and the Chocolate Sabotage

Thea Stilton and the Missing Myth

Thea Stilton and the Lost Letters

Thea Stilton and the Tropical Treasure

Thea Stilton and the Hollywood Hoax

Don't miss any of my fabumouse special editions!

THE JOURNEY
TO ATLANTIS

THE SECRET OF
THE FAIRIES

THE SECRET OF
THE SNOW

THE CLOUD
CASTLE

Be sure to read all my fabumouse adventures!

#1 Lost Treasure of the Emerald Eye

#2 The Curse of the Cheese Pyramid

#3 Cat and Mouse in a Haunted House

#4 I'm Too Fond of My Fur!

#5 Four Mice Deep in the Jungle

#6 Paws Off, Cheddarface!

#7 Red Pizzas for a Blue Count

#8 Attack of the Bandit Cats

#9 A Fabumouse Vacation for Geronimo

#10 All Because of a Cup of Coffee

#11 It's Halloween, You 'Fraidy Mouse!

#12 Merry Christmas, Geronimo!

#13 The Phantom of the Subway

#14 The Temple of the Ruby of Fire

#15 The Mona Mousa Code

#16 A Cheese-Colored Camper

#17 Watch Your Whiskers, Stilton!

#18 Shipwreck on the Pirate Islands

#19 My Name Is Stilton, Geronimo Stilton

#20 Surf's Up, Geronimo!

#21 The Wild, Wild West

#22 The Secret of Cacklefur Castle

A Christmas Tale

#23 Valentine's Day Disaster

#24 Field Trip to Niagara Falls

#25 The Search for Sunken Treasure

#26 The Mummy with No Name

#27 The Christmas Toy Factory

#28 Wedding Crasher

#29 Down and Out Down Under

#30 The Mouse Island Marathon

#31 The Mysterious Cheese Thief

Christmas Catastrophe

#32 Valley of the Giant Skeletons

#33 Geronimo and the Gold Medal Mystery

#34 Geronimo Stilton, Secret Agent

#35 A Very Merry Christmas

#36 Geronimo's Valentine

#37 The Race Across America

#38 A Fabumouse School Adventure

#39 Singing Sensation

#40 The Karate Mouse

#41 Mighty Mount Kilimanjaro

#42 The Peculiar Pumpkin Thief

#43 I'm Not a Supermouse!

#44 The Giant Diamond Robbery

#45 Save the White Whale!

#46 The Haunted Castle

#47 Run for the Hills, Geronimo!

#48 The Mystery in Venice

#49 The Way of the Samurai

#50 This Hotel Is Haunted!

#51 The Enormouse Pearl Heist

#52 Mouse in Space!

#53 Rumble in the Jungle

#54 Get into Gear, Stilton!

#55 The Golden Statue Plot

#56 Flight of the Red Bandit

The Hunt for the Golden Book

#57 The Stinky Cheese Vacation

#58 The Super Chef Contest

#59 Welcome to Moldy Manor

The Hunt for the Curious Cheese

#60 The Treasure of Easter Island

#61 Mouse House Hunter

#62 Mouse Overboard!

The Hunt for the Secret Papyrus

#63 The Cheese Experiment

Don't miss any of these Mouseford Academy adventures!

#1 Drama at Mouseford

#2 The Missing Diary

#3 Mouselets in Danger

#4 Dance Challenge

#5 The Secret Invention

#6 A Mouseford Musical

#7 Mice Take the Stage

#8 A Fashionable Mystery

#9 The Mysterious Love Letter

#10 A Dream on Ice

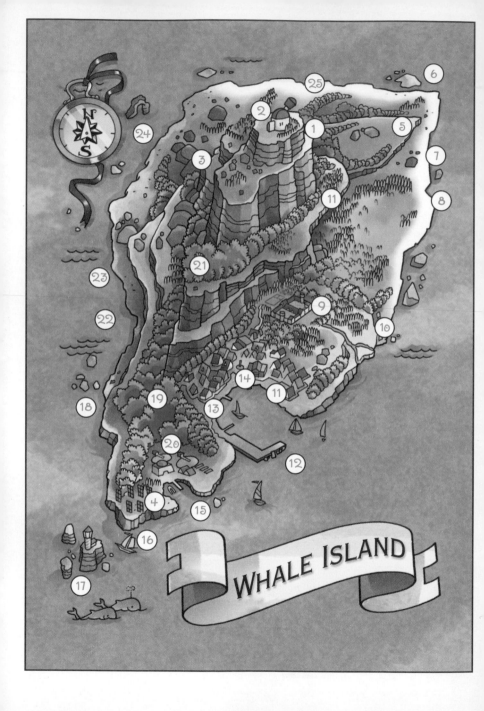

MAP OF WHALE ISLAND

1. Falcon Peak
2. Observatory
3. Mount Landslide
4. Solar Energy Plant
5. Ram Plain
6. Very Windy Point
7. Turtle Beach
8. Beachy Beach
9. Mouseford Academy
10. Kneecap River
11. Mariner's Inn
12. Port
13. Squid House
14. Town Square
15. Butterfly Bay
16. Mussel Point
17. Lighthouse Cliff
18. Pelican Cliff
19. Nightingale Woods
20. Marine Biology Lab
21. Hawk Woods
22. Windy Grotto
23. Seal Grotto
24. Seagulls Bay
25. Seashell Beach

THANKS FOR READING, AND GOOD-BYE UNTIL OUR NEXT MOUSEFORD ADVENTURE!